New Yeats Papers xv
General Editor : Liam Miller

M02 40000 18846

WITHDRAWN

PR 5908 P 6 F 37   48479

Farag, Fahmy

The Opposing Virtues

DATE DUE			
MAY 18 '89			

Waubonsee Community College

Fahmy Farag

The Opposing Virtues

two essays
Needless Horror or Terrible Beauty: Yeats's Ideas of Hatred, War, and Violence

W. B. Yeats and the Politics of *A Vision*

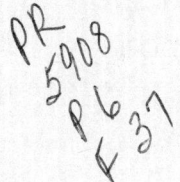

The Dolmen Press Dublin

Contents

Needless Horror or Terrible Beauty: Yeats's Ideas of Hatred, War, and Violence	page 5
W. B. Yeats and the Politics of *A Vision*	21
Appendix: Genealogical Tree of Revolution	50
Notes on the text	52

Acknowledgements

Grateful acknowledgement is made to Miss Anne Yeats, Senator Michael B. Yeats and The Macmillan Company for permission to quote the works and letters of W. B. Yeats; and to Professor A. N. Jeffares for permission to reproduce the 'Genealogical Tree of Revolution' from *W. B. Yeats, Man and Poet*. Thanks are also due to The Canada Council without whose support I should not have been able to undertake this research.

General Editor: Liam Miller

Set in Pilgrim type
and printed and published in the Republic of Ireland
at the Dolmen Press
North Richmond Industrial Estate, North Richmond Street, Dublin 1

First published 1978

ISBN 0 85105 323 8

Distributed in the United States of America and in Canada by
Humanities Press Inc.,
171 First Avenue, Atlantic Highlands, N.J. 07716

© Fahmy Farag 1978

Needless Horror or Terrible Beauty:
Yeats's Ideas of Hatred, War, and Violence

*I think that all noble things are the result of warfare;
great nations and classes, of warfare in the visible world,
great poetry and philosophy, of invisible warfare, the
division of a mind within itself, a victory, the sacrifice
of a man to himself.*

W. B. YEATS, *Essays*, p. 398

*We wish to grow peaceful crops, but we must dig our
furrows with the sword.*

W. B. YEATS, *Explorations*, p. 83

Yeats's contradictory and often paradoxical attitudes to hatred, violence, and war, and his seemingly incongruous use of these terms in his prose and poetry, have always baffled and bewildered even the most devoted Yeatsians. The poet, for example, condemns hatred in many of his poems and public utterances, but tends at times to accept it as a positive and creative force. In 'A Prayer for My Daughter' he warns against the 'arrogance and hatred . . . Peddled in the thoroughfares', and argues that 'to be choked with hate/ May well be of all evil chances chief'.[1] However, in 'Ribh Considers Christian Love Insufficient', he asserts that he studies 'hatred with great diligence', for 'hatred of God may bring the soul to God'.[2] In 'The Circus Animals' Desertion', and 'No Second Troy' he recalls how Maud Gonne filled his days with misery when she 'taught to ignorant men most violent ways'; she 'must her own soul destroy' for 'fanaticism and hate enslave it'.[3] In sharp contrast with this is his account in *The Tables of the Law* of how 'Jonathan Swift made a soul for the gentlemen of this city [Dublin] by hating his neighbour as himself',[4] or with his declaration in the second part of 'Under Ben Bulben' of the necessity of violence in human affairs.

His attitude to war and warfare is even more paradoxical. He expresses unmitigated horror at the murder and bloodshed that swept Ireland during the Black and Tan war:

> Now days are dragon-ridden, the nightmare
> Rides upon sleep: a drunken soldiery
> Can leave the mother, murdered at her door,
> To crawl in her own blood, and go scot-free . . .[5]

Despite his obvious revulsion to 'the growing murderousness of the world' in 'Meditations in Time of Civil War', 'Nineteen Hundred and Nineteen', and 'The Man and the Echo', he is reported, when asked for a message to India, whose wisdom he loved and admired, to have unsheathed Sato's sword and shouted, 'Let 100,000 men of one side meet the other. That is my message to India . . . Conflict, more conflict.'[6] In 1915 he was asked for a war poem, but he did not find the prospect of carnage and catastrophe particularly inspiring; he could only say, 'I shall keep the neighbourhood of the seven sleepers of Ephesus, hoping to catch their comfortable snores till this bloody frivolity is over.'[7] It is certainly difficult to reconcile this with the Yeats who, a few years earlier, endorsed with great satisfaction the Heraclitean doctrine of creative conflict: 'War is the father of all and the king of all, and some he has made gods and some men, some bound and some free.'[8] As a matter of fact, he calls openly and unabashedly for war both in *A Vision* and in *On the Boiler*; 'love war because of its horror that belief may be changed, civilization renewed';⁹ or again, 'prepare for war, prepare your children and all that you can reach, for how can a nation or a kindred without war become that "bright particular star" of Shakespeare.' ¹⁰ All this, however, seems unaccountably inconsistent with his rhetorical denunciation of war and his compassionate treatment of its victims in 'Reprisals':

> Where may new-married women sit
> And suckle children now? Armed men
> May murder them in passing by
> Nor law nor parliament take heed.¹¹

Faced with this confusing mixture, Yeatsian scholars have done their best either to ignore these troublesome paradoxes or, when pressed, to apologize for them by speculating vaguely on old age, on the effect of the Steinach operation, or some such disingenuous excuse. On the other hand, the disapproving critics emphasise that his attitudes to violence, hatred, and war are not susceptible to too close analysis and should not occasion confusion or puzzlement. To them, he is an autocrat, an avowed Fascist who wrote marching songs for the Irish Blueshirts. However, it is time, now that the importance of the poet's occult involvement is beginning to receive its proper emphasis, to set aside rancorous or defensive criticism of Yeats and try and reinterpret these shifting attitudes in the context of his mystical and esoteric beliefs. This paper is, in fact, an attempt to emphasise first and mainly our failure to see that the poet's ambivalence is firmly anchored in his training as a Cabbalist; and secondly, to clarify his nomenclature with reference to a range of connotative values which may hitherto have escaped our attention.

It should be made clear at the start that Yeats's notions of war and violence bear little or no relation to those of the jingoists, the colonialists, or the war-mongering Fascists. They evolved in all likelihood from his study of Blake and Vico, from his acquaintance with Madame Blavatsky and MacGregor Mathers, and, above all, from his experience and training in The Order of the Golden Dawn. Varied and pluralistic as these studies may seem, they are essentially based on a common dialectic that postulates the antinomial nature of all energy in the universe. Conflict, war, and violence, being forms of energy, are integral to the tension between opposites that make progression towards harmony and peace possible. Yeats's first encounter with the distinction between the benevolent and malevolent aspects of energy occurred when he and Edwin Ellis edited their three-volume edition of Blake. In his introduction to the book, Yeats writes, 'he [Blake] saw in every issue the whole contest of light and darkness, and found no peace . . . in every atom of dust, Los, the "eternal mind", warred upon dragon Urizen, "the God of this World." ' [12] Indeed, Blake explains in *Jerusalem* that war and hunting are 'the two sources of life in eternity' but when they are distorted they become the 'sources of dark and bitter death and corroding hell' (38 : 31-32).

Love and Hate, are necessary to Human existence. From these Contraries spring what the religions call Good and Evil. Good is the passive that obeys Reason. Evil is the active springing from Energy.[13]

The energetic communal conflicts and wars which Albion fears and labels 'sin' are creative, not destructive: 'our wars are wars of life, and wounds of love' (34 : 14). And the crucifixion of Luvah by which his heart is ripped away is elevated to the arrows of love that 'open the hidden Heart in Wars of mutual Benevolence, Wars of Love' (97 : 14). Yeats himself explains: 'Blake has said that "the roaring of lions, the howling of wolves, the raging of the stormy sea, and the destructive sword are portions of Eternity, too great for the eye of man." ' [14] Similarly, Yeats, as will be shown later in the discussion, came to associate the 'murderous innocence of the sea', 'the odour of blood', 'Sato's Sword', and the 'rough beast' of 'The Second Coming' with the primary, physical world of the flesh, particularly in its relation to the spiritual world and the cycles of history.

As a member of The Hermetic Order of the Golden Dawn for more than thirty years, Yeats's mind was imbued with the doctrine that all energy in the universe is double-natured, with benign as well as malign attributes; it is both creative and destructive, primary and antithetical. As a neophyte, he was given the name *Demon Est Deus Inversus*, and taught that the dialectic nature of the Tree of Life symbolises the warring opposites whose conflict makes all life possible. All existence is 'an open or veiled struggle of life against life, of number against number, and all the numbers against unity.' [15] In 'The Two Trees', Yeats describes the antithetical nature of the Sephirotic Tree; on one side the beneficent *Sephiroth*, on the other the dread *Qlippoth*. From then on, Yeats's interest in the 'clashing of swords' — far from being bloodthirsty — acquired certain mystical and esoteric connotations. To his ears, and to those of his fellow occultists, it became the music that proclaimed the marriage of heaven and hell:

> I made a certain girl see a vision of the Garden of Eden. She heard "the music of Paradise coming from the Tree of Life," and, when I told her to put her ear against the bark, that she might hear the better, found that it was made by the continuous clashing of swords.[16]

His poem 'Vacillation' opens with a succinct restatement of Blake's theory of contraries followed by a vivid description of the ceaseless battle between the two aspects of reality; the 'staring fury' and 'the blind lush leaf' destroy and recreate themselves:

> A tree there is that from its topmost bough
> Is half all glittering flame and half all green . . .
> And half and half consume what they renew . . .[17]

The Cabbalists and the occultists of the nineties believed that the golden dawn of the world's rebirth and the coming of the new avatar would be preceded by a universal and devastating war. Madame Blavatsky explained to her disciples who aspired for a new 'spiritual age' that Europe was on the eve of a cataclysm which her own cycle of racial Karma had led her to. And MacGregor Mathers, Yeats's master in The Hermetic Order — as reported by the poet himself — was exclusively interested in 'magic and the theory of war, for he believed himself a born commander and all but equal in wisdom and in power to that Old Jew. . . .'[18] He talked continually from about 1893 on of the 'imminence of immense wars', and taught his fellow Cabbalists that

> the fifth enumeration, Power or Might . . . is a symbol of creative power and force. Its planetary attribution is Mars, its quality being that destructive force which demolishes all forms . . . when their term of usefulness and healthy life is done. It symbolises not so much a fixed state of things, as an act, a further passage and transition of potentiality into actuality.[19]

Mathers explained the well-known symbol of a serpent holding his tail in his mouth as 'the executor of judgment . . . the destroyer . . . [who] is not called into action till justice requires him.'[20]

Soon after his acquaintance with Mathers, Yeats reported that mediums and clairvoyants everywhere were predicting the same destructive wars, and he even went so far as to collect 'the prophecies of various countries on the subject'.[21] The poet seriously believed that the present cycle of civilization was about to reverse itself, and he wrote at the time to Florence Farr, a fellow occultist, asking her if the 'magical armageddon' was about to begin, and added that 'the war would fulfil the prophets and especially a prophetic vision I had . . . with the Mathers's, and so far be for the glory of God but what a dusk of nations it would be? for surely it would drag in half the world.'[22] In July 1896, William Horton, a close friend of the poet, wrote to him, 'My art is and will continue to be as it were my *receptive, peaceful* . . . work. But my *Active Work* — I mean work that will affect people, principalities, and powers — is not yet. What the Work will be I cannot say now but that the Work will come by and bye I feel sure and think it will be connected with leadership in *Spiritual Warfare.*'[23]

It is little wonder, therefore, that Yeats's sense that the world was awaiting a revelation that would violently destroy all things and bring a different order to birth, found expression in some of his early work. For example, all the stories that form the substance of *The Secret Rose* (1897), though written at different times and in different styles have, as Yeats indicated in his Dedication to the first edition, 'but one subject, the war of the spiritual with the natural order'. And in *The Wind Among the Reeds*, the poet cries out for the destruction of the material world, and announces the imminence of a new age:

> . . . I, too, await
> The hour of thy great wind of love and hate . . .
> Surely thine hour has come, thy great wind blows,
> Far-off, most secret, and inviolate Rose?[24]

The most forceful apocalyptic poem in this volume, however, is 'The Valley of the Black Pig': 'unknown spears/Suddenly hurtle before my dream-awakened eyes,/And then the clash of fallen horsemen and the cries/Of unknown perishing armies beat about my ears.'[25]

In a letter to A. H. Bullen, Yeats explains that his plays *Where There is Nothing, There is God* and *The Unicorn From the Stars* 'carry to a more complete realization the central idea of the stories of *The Secret Rose.*'[26] In *Where There is Nothing*, Paul Ruttledge, the character representing the spiritual world, becomes the rough beast that will pull down the material world and bring it to an end:

Sometimes I dream I am pulling down . . . the whole world . . . I would like to have great iron claws, and to put them about the pillars, and to pull and pull till everything fell into pieces.[27]

He argues that the saints always fight, 'for their hand is against the world', and adds:

I want the happiness of men who fight . . . not the fighting of men in red coats, that formal, soon-finished fighting, but the endless battle, the endless battle.[28]

In *The Unicorn from The Stars* the apocalyptic agent becomes the unicorn, the symbol for a divine force working within the soul and manifested in the moment of inspiration, of joyous vision, that will bring renewal with destruction. It should be remembered that the title for the third grade of the Order of the Golden Dawn, which the poet himself held for some time in the early 'nineties, was that of *Monoceros de Astris*, the Unicorn from the Stars. At any rate, Martin Hearne, the prototype of Paul Ruttledge in the earlier version of the play, preaches that 'the battle goes on always, always. That is the joy of Heaven, continual battle',[29] and associates raging violence and newborn joy, tragedy and laughter in instantaneous synthesis. Man is engaged in a ceaseless battle within himself and with the world of time — a battle that will be lost and won when he burns up everything, and where there is nothing, there is God.

The golden dawn of the world's rebirth was, of course, closely associated with the individual's transmutation. Blake and the Cabbalists considered man to be a microcosm, and the double-natured tree was also seen as a picture of human nature; it is both divine and brutal. Yeats's Golden Dawn name, *Demon Est Deus Inversus*, was doubtless a constant reminder that if God carries or implies his opposite, man too has to contend with his antagonist. The poet, as a matter of fact, describes in *A Vision* the four faculties of man as 'alternately shield and sword'[30] and even his saint is an archer who 'shoots an arrow from the burning bow'.

The human mind, therefore, is the battleground of man and daimon, and the outcome of this tragic war is the heroic choice that shapes and is the cause of the war that ensues between man and his age. If we reject the brutal aspect of man and ignore his tragic war with himself and the world, we are bound to lose what Yeats calls the 'Vision of Evil', and 'cherish [some] species of optimism,' some kind of false beauty:

Shelley out of phase writes pamphlets, and dreams of converting the world . . . and yet . . . how subject he is to nightmare! He sees the devil leaning against a tree, is attacked by imaginary assassins. . . . Dante . . . saw all things set in order . . . and was content to see both good and evil. Shelley, upon the other hand . . . lacked the Vision of Evil, could not conceive of the world as a continual conflict. . . . Being out of phase he [tried] to evade hatred, or rather to hide it from his own eyes.[31]

Yeats, on the other hand, considers Lionel Johnson a great religious poet who 'made his poetry out of the struggle with his own soul which the sword of Fate had as it were divided in two',[32] and argues that all the great things of life have come from battle:

I do not think any nature comes to the self-knowledge that is genius without the original evil which gives the antagonist in that battle whose spoil and monument is knowledge. He emits to evil in gathering darkness a genius which was in its heart of hearts essentially joyous.[33]

Yeats is aware of the danger to literature brought about by those who pursue or quest after the purely spiritual or ideal alone. They usually miss the violence and the brutality of the flesh which makes both life and literature heroic, forceful, and tragic. The poet is equally aware that if public institutions fail to recognize man's violence, this violence can only find free play in the anonymous violence of public opinion:

If human violence is not embodied in our institutions, the young will not give them their affection, nor the young and old their loyalty.[34]

In a public speech in 1924, he scoffed at the facile and shallow optimism of those who dreamt that early in the twentieth century war would have come to an end, and before the middle of the century there would be no more poverty: ' "There will never be another war," that was the opium dream. That is all gone. . . . We do not believe that war is passing away, and we are not certain that the world is growing better.'[35] He expresses the same belief in 'Nineteen Hundred and Nineteen';

> O what fine thought we had because we thought
> That the worst rogues and rascals had died out.
> All teeth were drawn, all ancient tricks unlearned,
> And a great army but a showy thing. . . .
> We pieced our thoughts into philosophy,
> And planned to bring the world under a rule,
> Who are but weasels fighting in a hole.[36]

In the first section of 'Meditations in Time of Civil War', Yeats links greatness with violence. The noble Irish houses and buildings came from the power, the violence, and the arrogance that was determined to

> rear in stone
> The sweetness that all longed for night and day,
> The gentleness none there had ever known.[37]

The ancient and stately homes may seem solitary and peaceful, but they are founded by passions of military men. Their apparent delicacy and quiet can only be understood as the mask hiding the true savagery of their foundation and history. Through union with the opposite of everything they were, the bitter, turbulent men that built them had turned their brutal and destructive instincts into civilized achievement. In this poem, Yeats seems for a moment to contemplate the violence of the Irish Civil War as a possible prelude to a period of greatness, harmony, and peace. This contemplation, however, gives way, in the final sections of the poem, to a disappointed and disillusioned realization that this war is not of the creative variety he hopes for:

> We had fed the heart on fantasies,
> The heart's grown brutal from the fare;
> More substance in our enmities
> Than in our love . . .[38]

Many commentators claim that in some of these poems Yeats skates dangerously close to the Fascist and Nazi ideas of war and violence, and partly attribute this to the influence of Nietzsche on the poet. Apparently, they find evidence to support their theories in Yeats's use of the terminology of 'fierce, exuberant, world-affirming', and 'war-tested' heroes. These critics, however, might be a little surprised to discover that Yeats's mystical vision linked war, love, and wisdom as early as *The Wanderings of Oisin* (1888), *The Shadowy Waters* (1900), and 'The Gift of Harun Al-Rashid' (1923). For example, the poet in *The Wanderings of Oisin* throws in his lot with Oisin (the swordsman) rather than with St. Patrick. Oisin who 'for a hundred years/So warred, so feasted', realizes in old age that war is requisite to the fulfilment of the creative self, and craves nothing except 'an endless feast, and endless war'.[39] And in *On Baile's Strand*, Cuchulain, as if in answer to Oisin's cry, says:

> No wonder in that, no wonder at all in that.
> I never have known love but as a kiss
> In the mid-battle, and a difficult truce . . .
> A brief forgiveness between opposites
> That have been hatreds for three times the age
> Of this long-'stablished ground.[40]

In *The Shadowy Waters* Forgael declares that 'love is war, and there is hatred in it.'[41] In 'The Gift of Harun Al-Rashid', Kusta Ben Luka discerns behind the confusion and 'the embroidery' of love, the never-ending war between man and daimon, for the love of man and woman is an image of that warfare, and 'sexual love is based on spiritual hate':[42]

> A woman's beauty is a storm-tossed banner;
> Under it wisdom stands, and I alone —
> Of all Arabia's lovers I alone —
> Nor dazzled by the embroidery, nor lost
> In the confusion of its night-dark folds,
> Can hear the armed man speak.[43]

Wisdom is 'the armed man' who can only express himself through sexual love and the clash of swords.

With the development of the system of *A Vision*, Yeats's preoccupation with things 'emblematic of love and war' becomes the focus of his life and work. The central tenet of his philosophy becomes war within the self and all things which is necessary for growth towards harmony, beauty, and fulfilment. In fact, fighting becomes for the poet the exemplary relationship between man and his ideal selfhood, his subjectivity, his antithesis, and his beloved; all these being opposite of his natural self. A dramatic expression of this theme is found in the Cuchulain plays where heroic love, war, and wisdom are fused together in a knot of concentrated power. The warrior theme in the plays is cunningly dependent on Cuchulain's spiritual adventures as lover and his search for wisdom and completeness.

Yeats's interpretation of the history of civilization in terms of antithesis and warfare has been sufficiently and systematically explored. Suffice it to say that in his panoramic view of history, he conceives of 'love and war' as the irreconcilable but indivisible energy behind both *Antithetical* and *Primary* civilizations:

I imagine the annunciation that founded Greece as made to Leda, remembering that they showed in a Spartan temple . . . an unhatched egg of hers; and that from one of her eggs came Love and from the other War. But all things are from antithesis. . . .[44]

In 'Leda and the Swan' the moment of revelation may be brutal and violent, but it brings a new order, a new civilization. This civilization contains in its turn the germ of its own destruction:

> A shudder in the loins engenders there
> The broken wall, the burning roof and tower
> And Agamemnon dead.[45]

The Christian dispensation may have thrown out the values of the Graeco-Roman civilization, but the Christian God of Love, nevertheless, is resurrected under the sign of war: 'Christ rose from the dead at a full moon in the first month of the year, the month that we have named from Mars.'[46] At the end of the present cycle the old *Primary* will 'become the new *Antithetical*, the old subconscious turbulent instinct'. The world of rigid custom and law will be broken by 'the uncontrollable mystery upon the bestial floor',[47] the rough beast of 'The Second Coming'. The next cycle will then be initiated by

Some Asiatic Nation [that] would base its whole civilization upon War, that its governing class would take care of the common people as our governing class could not or would not, that they might obey in War and be loyal in defeat. That its Schools and Universities would . . . [prepare] all to face death without flinching, perhaps even with joy. As according to their philosophy the dead will not pass to a remote Heaven, but return to the Earth, it will seem as though the soldier's dead body manured the fields he himself would till.[48]

War, violence, and death are feared by those who live solely for the senses and the body, and those who believe in one earthly life. Death is welcomed, however, by those whose mental eyes have been awakened to the spiritual truth and the beauty that lie beyond the world and for which they can become a medium during their mortal lives: 'Death is the last adventure, the first perfect joy, for at death the soul comes into possession of itself, and returns to the joy that made it.'[49] It is this enlargement of vision that 'changed utterly' the heroes of 'Easter 1916'; they achieved 'terrible beauty' in their violent encounter with their heroic opposites:

> . . . they dreamed and are dead;
> And what if excess of love
> Bewildered them till they died?

It is this enlarged vision which keeps the poets and the artists gay in the face of tragedy. They know that their civilization must be 'put to the sword', and that 'they and their wisdom [must go] to rack', but they face death without hysteria; they accept their doom serenely, even gaily, because

> All things fall and are built again,
> And those that build them again are gay.[50]

The ceaseless battle that man and civilization have to wage as they pass through nature to eternity is summed up with splendid conciseness in 'The Four Ages of Man':

> He with body waged a fight,
> But body won; it walks upright.
>
> Then he struggled with the heart;
> Innocence and peace depart.
>
> Then he struggled with the mind;
> His proud heart he left behind.
>
> Now his wars on God begin;
> At stroke of midnight God shall win.[51]

God Himself is man's opponent, and the final struggle is with Him, whether He keeps His own shape or takes that of death or destiny. The war on God, therefore, is the ultimate heroism, and like all heroism in Yeats ends in defeat.

*

There is ample evidence that Yeats developed, early in life, a dual attitude to war and violence. In 'The Trembling of the Veil', for example, he recounts how Maud Gonne vexed his father when she first met him in 1889 'by praising war, war for its own sake, not as the creator of certain virtues'.[52] And, towards the end of his life, he draws a clear distinction between creative and wanton destruction. He repudiates 'corporeal', anonymous war which modern historians explain as a reasoned conflict based on material interests,[53] and endorses 'that other war, where opposites die each other's death'.[54] For him, war, violence, conflict and hatred are terms of condemnation when used as *negatives*, but terms of praise when used as *contraries*. As negatives they are the source of meaningless suffering and spiritual death:

> The rage-driven, rage-tormented, and rage-hungry troop,
> Trooper belabouring trooper, biting at arm or at face,
> Plunges towards nothing, arms and fingers spreading wide
> For the embrace of nothing. . . .[55]

Senseless violence triggered by bigotry or intolerance is a crime against civilization itself:

> Incendiary or bigot could be found
> To burn that stump on the Acropolis,
> Or break in bits the famous ivories
> Or traffic in the grasshoppers or bees. . . .[56]

A 'primary' battle, taking place outside the character of man or nation is futile and frivolous. War and violence can only be significant if they are the means by which the two halves of the personality are brought together. In that sense, terror, hatred and destruction are justifiable elements in the spiritual transformation that takes place as a result of the union with the opposite and partner to whatever is creative in man or civilization. Yeats's view can best be illustrated by his rejection in the 'thirties of O'Casey's play *The Silver Tassie*:

When the directors of the Abbey Theatre rejected *The Silver Tassie* they did so because they thought it a bad play and a play which would mar the fame and popularity of its writer. . . . The war, as O'Casey has conceived it, is an equivalent for those primary qualities brought down by Berkeley's Secret Society, it stands outside the characters, it is not part of their expression. . . . The English critics feel differently, to them a theme that "bulks largely in the news" gives dignity to human nature. . . . We on the other hand are certain that nothing can give dignity to human nature but the character and energy of its expression.[57]

To be a passive participant in war, to suffer without any affirmative role repelled and exasperated him. As editor of *The Oxford Book of Modern Verse* (1892-1935), he refused to include the War Poets because 'passive suffering is not a theme for poetry'. Primary violence deals only with the surface of life and its end is necessarily material and mechanical:

> Hurrah for revolution and more cannon-shot!
> A beggar upon horseback lashes a beggar on foot.
> Hurrah for revolution and cannon come again!
> The beggars have changed places, but the lash goes on.[58]

Yeats argues that 'the sense of spiritual reality comes . . . to the individual or to crowds from some violent shock.'[59] This shock can sometimes create the circumstances by which a man can be brought face to face with his buried self:

> You that Mitchel's prayer have heard,
> "Send war in our time, O Lord!"
> Know that when all words are said
> And a man is fighting mad,
> Something drops from eyes long blind,
> He completes his partial mind,
> For an instant stands at ease,
> Laughs aloud, his heart at peace.
> Even the wisest man grows tense
> With some sort of violence
> Before he can accomplish fate,
> Know his work or choose his mate.[60]

As death threatens, man is lifted out of the confusion of external circumstances and the accident of individuality and becomes part of the eternal design.

The poet's study of the esoteric sciences taught him that just as common metals can be transmuted into gold when subjected to the alchemical fire, the human soul can, on the metaphysical level, be transformed into an imperishable spirit. To him, then, war, hatred, and violence are images of that purifying fire that may put the trivial daily self in touch with the eternal self and effect the spiritual regeneration of a man or nation:

> . . . the Gate-Keepers who drive the nation to war or anarchy that it may find its Image are different from those who drive individual men, though I think at times they work together.[61]

Just as the individual who seeks perfection of life through Unity of Being has to accept the tragic war with his anti-self, a nation that pursues wisdom through Unity of Culture must submit to the transforming fire. As a matter of fact, the poet asserts that 'the "Irishry" have preserved their ancient "deposit" through wars',[62] and avers that all creation is from conflict, whether with our own minds or with those of others, and 'the historian who dreams of bloodless victory, wrongs the wounded veterans'.[63] At the end of his life, he exhorts his countrymen to bring up their children on an education of arms and letters in the hope that this kind of training and discipline may enable them to 'throw back from [their] shores the . . . uneducated masses of the commercial nations'[64] and win an 'Irish Salamis' that may usher in the new antithetical dispensation.

W. B. Yeats and the Politics of *A Vision*

... politics, for the vision-seeking man, can be but half achievement, a choice of an almost easy kind of skill instead of that kind which is, of all those not impossible, the most difficult.

In his celebrated elegy, 'In Memory of W. B. Yeats', Auden declares:

> Time that is intolerant
> Of the brave and innocent
> And indifferent in a week
> To a beautiful physique,
> Worships language and forgives
> Everyone by whom it lives. . . .
>
> Time that with this strange excuse
> Pardoned Kipling and his views,
> And will pardon Paul Claudel,
> Pardons him for writing well.

Time has indeed diminished our interest in the political views of Kipling and Claudel, but the politics of Yeats seem to defy Auden's prediction and to resist the normal therapeutic effect of time. The attack on Yeats's aristocratic leanings and his so-called sinister political theories was formally launched by MacNeice[1] in 1941 and continued unabated through the 'fifties and the 'sixties, culminating in the famous article of Conor Cruise O'Brien.[2] More recently, a spate of publications by William Thompson, John Harrison, Donald Torchiana, Hazard Adams, Malcolm Brown and others have dealt with Yeats's politics with varying degree of success, depending on how closely these authors view the Irish context of his attitudes. In the exchange between Yeats's defenders and detractors, terms like 'Fascist' and 'proto-Fascist' are still being frequently heard. Such charges seem to be the unpleasant legacy of the Second World War, a time when the democratic countries were massively challenged by authoritarian regimes, a time when writers and intellectuals were crudely classified according to simple criteria that recognize no grey areas and no fine distinctions. In a war of survival, nations are hardly expected to tolerate those who refuse to flaunt their political badges or draw their opinions from newspaper editorials. It is easy, therefore, to explain and understand why many of the great literary figures who rejected political conformity in the 'thirties were branded before and during the war. Authors of different persuasions like D. H. Lawrence, Wyndham Lewis, T. S. Eliot, Aldous Huxley, and Yeats were often stigmatized as 'fascists', 'reactionaries', 'traitors', etc. Unfortunately, some of these labels have been allowed to harden into permanent classifications when the challenge has disappeared and the danger has receded. The problem in the case of Yeats has certainly been compounded by the fact that his death coincided with the outbreak of the war, which removed the chance of self-explanation and made a re-examination of his record in the postwar era an academic rather than a public concern. To complicate matters still further, the national and religious struggle in Ireland has not yet been resolved and partisan politics have made any cool presentation of evidence in defence of Yeats, within the Irish context, almost impossible.

This essay is an attempt to emphasize first and mainly our failure to see a coherence in Yeats's political views and to understand how Ireland and Europe must have appeared to a man possessed of a highly individual philosophy of history; and secondly, to question the validity of using vague, imprecise political terms in any interpretation of his works.

Yeats's view of history and politics is more spiritual than many people think, and his hopes and attempts to unify Ireland spiritually take precedence over any other consideration. From the beginning he identified Irish politics with his own interests and desires: his own hope for the restoration of an imaginative, heroic, subjective, legendary and religious state. In the introduction to *The Secret Rose* he argues that so far as his work is visionary it is Irish, and insists that his hermetic interests place him all the more in the pure Irish tradition.[3] This led him in 1897 to found an Irish Mystical Order in the hope of marrying national politics to esoteric religions in order to effect the spiritual regeneration of the modern Celt. He wanted, as he tells us in *The Words Upon the Window Pane*, to free the Irish imagination from practical politics, from political enmity, and to turn it to imaginative nationalism, to Gaelic, to the ancient stories, and to lyrical poetry and to drama.[4] To Yeats, politics implied an attitude towards this world and the next: he believed that the real nation is where its soul is, and the soul of a nation is the men who have attained unto themselves. Only in being true to his genius can a man be true to his race, and whenever a man has found himself, the purpose of nationality is fulfilled in him. A man 'must brood over his work so long and so unbrokenly that he find there all his patriotism, all his passion, his religion even . . . until at last he can cry with Paracelsus, "In this crust of bread I have found all the stars and all the heavens." '[5]

There is little doubt that Yeats saw himself as the leader of an esoteric and supra-mundane nationalist movement which was not political, but whose success depended in some degree upon the preservation of the heroic attitude in Irish politics — an attitude which could not be maintained, he believed, unless it was rooted in contemplation. He even hoped at one point to introduce *A Vision* directly into the political scene; 'if readers would master [my] system,' he wrote, 'the curtain may ring up on a new drama.' Perhaps some 'new conspiracy might be fomented which would better embody [my] ideas than any existing institution or organization.'[6] And a few months before his death, he warned his countrymen: 'Do not try to pour Ireland into any political system. Think first how many able men . . . the country has, how many it can hope to have in the near future, and mould your system upon those men. . . . Republics, Kingdoms, Soviets, Corporate States, Parliaments, are trash. . . . These men, whether six or six thousand, are the core of Ireland, are Ireland itself.'[7]

He approached history and politics, as he explained in one of his letters, with literary eyes and tried to 'turn all into a kind of theatre.'[8] He saw Irish nationalism in terms of myth and image, and thought of the Literary Revival as a cultural and spiritual movement basically opposed to politics. 'In my savage youth,' he wrote, 'I was accustomed to say that no man should be permitted to open his mouth in Parliament until he had sung or written his Utopia, for lacking that we could not know where he was taking us. . . .'[9] And in describing the tours of the Abbey Theatre in 1938, he asserted that 'These tours, and Irish songs and novels, when they come from a deeper life than their nineteenth century predecessors, are taking the place of political speakers, political organizations, in holding together the twenty scattered millions conscious of their Irish blood.'[10] For him the terms 'politics' and 'politicians' meant an activity in support of abstract ideas and implied an indulgence in hatred and bitterness:

> A Statesman is an easy man,
> He tells his lies by rote;
> A journalist makes up his lies
> And takes you by the throat.[11]

But, seen through his art, politics fundamentally implied an arduous search for the nation's image as it existed in *Anima mundi*.

His literary movement was, then, political and nationalist only in the sense that it was an instrument in a campaign to revitalize the culture of the nation, to stem the filthy modern tide of materialism, to gear the energies of the country to the grand design of the preordained historical cycles as he envisaged them in *A Vision*. 'I am no Nationalist, except in Ireland for passing reasons,' he declared, 'State and Nation are the work of intellect, and when you consider what comes before and after them they are . . . not worth the blade of grass God gives for the nest of the linnet.'[12] He believed that the revolt of the soul against the intellect was beginning in the world, and that the arts should take upon their shoulders the burdens that have fallen from the shoulders of priests, and lead us back upon our journey by filling our thoughts with the essence of things, and not with things.[13] As Frank O'Connor has aptly pointed out, 'All his blunderings in religion, philosophy and politics were part of a quest for that "religion of the whole world"; for some ancient unity which he believed had once existed, and he saw in the development of civilization only the breaking up into smaller and smaller fragments of what had once been complete. . . .'.[14]

In dealing with Yeats's politics, we should never lose sight of his mythic over-view of the world and interpret his activities merely in terms of local quarrels. His politics are certainly an attempt to capture something larger than the turbulent, partisan disputes which plagued Ireland during his lifetime. His double vision gave him two perspectives on reality and hence he could say, in a moment of paradoxical synthesis, 'History seems to me a human drama, keeping the classical unities by the clear division of its epochs, turning one way or the other because this man hates or that man loves. . . . Yet the drama has its plot, and this plot ordained character and passions and exists for their sake.'[15] In other words, our everyday clashes and accords, our local events and minor disputes, with all the passions they generate and the feelings they engender, constitute the more distant drama of preordained history with its divisions and dispensations. Life is not exactly in our control, for we enact in our daily lives a drama in which higher beings make use of our bodies and our passions. And when he writes, 'I am full of uncertainty, not knowing when I am the finger, when the clay,'[16] he is aware that the artist's business is to become the vehicle for the transmission of ultimate truth, prophecy, or those emotions which have a superhuman referent.

*

Yeats's antinomial approach to reality has been sufficiently and systematically explored in relation to his poetic imagination, but little has been done to relate it seriously to his politics. His ever-changing views, his paradoxical utterances, and his self-contradictions cannot be ignored in any appraisal of his social or political beliefs. It is precisely these opposite patterns of thought and feeling, existing side by side, which have provided his commentators with every opportunity to employ, consciously or unconsciously, the type of selective perception and partial approach that usually characterises one-sided criticism. Determined to see in his double consciousness of reality a duplicity fed by a calculating mind, these commentators pick out, like looting soldiers, what little they can use, and soil and confuse the rest.

To understand the contours of Yeats's politics, it is necessary to grasp the indissoluble relationship between his Golden Dawn training and what might be called his political stance. The organization, as well as the occult doctrines of the Order, provides a structural framework for his social and political faith, and unless we are willing to accept the basic antinomial philosophy implied in his Golden Dawn name — *Demon Est Deus Inversus* — as integral to his personal and political life, we shall fail to see any coherence in his seemingly incongruous statements and attitudes. His interest in the twin aspects of reality and his understanding of history and politics can only be explained with reference to the idea of eternal recurrence, and an inclusive vision based on the tension between opposites:

> Why must I think the victorious cause the better? Why should Mommsen think the less of Cicero because Caesar beat him? I am satisfied, the Platonic Year in my head, to find but drama. I prefer that the defeated cause should be more vividly described than that which has the advertisement of victory. No battle has been finally won or lost. . . .[17]

The qualities that creatively oppose or are missing from a man's or a nation's personality are what he calls in *Anima Hominis* 'the opposing virtues'. Only the greatest obstacle 'that can be contemplated without despair rouses the will to full intensity'.[18] A nation is continually fighting a battle against fate; it is divided against itself and has no choice but to struggle unceasingly to regain its lost unity — a unity which can only be attained by seeking everything that is different from what it actually is in daily life. Yeats feels that his is the unpopular duty to challenge his country to find 'the opposing virtues', and to encourage his countrymen to complete themselves by embracing their anti-selves. Has not the intellect of Ireland always found itself instinctively through a similar process?

> . . . Berkeley with his belief in perception, that abstract ideas are mere words, Swift with his love of perfect nature . . . his disbelief in Newton's system and every sort of machine, Goldsmith and his delight in the particulars of common life that shocked his contemporaries, Burke with his conviction that all States not grown slowly like a forest tree are tyrannies, *found in England the opposite that stung their own thought into expression and made it lucid.* [Italics mine][19]

The nationalist poet, he believes, should follow the butterfly of his genius and not the gloomy bird of prey of his fellow-citizens' preconceived ideas. His duty is to create 'personages and lyric emotions which startle [them] by being at once bizarre and an image of [their] own secret thoughts.'[20]

If he really achieve the miracle, if he really make all that he has seen and felt and known a portion of his own intense nature, if he puts it all into the fire of his energy, *he need not fear being a stranger among his own people in the end. There never have been men more unlike an Englishman's idea of himself than Keats and Shelley*, while Campbell, whose emotion came out of a shallow well, was very like that idea. *We call certain minds creative because they are among the moulders of their nation and are not made upon its mould*, and they resemble one another in this only — they have never been foreknown or fulfilled an expectation. [Italics mine][21]

True to his Cabbalist training, Yeats declares that the artist 'is known from other men by making all he handles like himself, and yet by the unlikeness to himself, of all that comes before him in a pure contemplation.'[22]

Nations, races, and individual men, if they are to attain 'active virtue', as distinguished from the passive acceptance of a code, must imagine themselves as different from what they are in actual life, and impose a discipline upon themselves. In seeking their anti-selves, they find the daimon that feeds the secret hunger in their hearts by setting them, paradoxically, to the hardest work among those not impossible. There is therefore a deep enmity between a nation and its destiny, and yet a nation loves nothing but its destiny. Because the national poet is moulded by influences that are secretly moulding his country, and because his role is to express through the 'Unity of Image' his country's destiny, he may be driven out by his countrymen, and though he may live in exile for many years, he is accepted by them in the end. Yeats explains in 1938 that the great artists cannot accept 'dominant opinion' for they are the 'opposites of their time':[23]

Wherever young men gather together all over Ireland they are discussing such questions as the virtues of the Irish people, how much they are slandered by England, and so on. Scotland in the eighteenth century got into an attitude of the same kind, which resulted in a condition of gloom. A poet came to destroy that attitude of mind. Instead of celebrating piety and like things he celebrated drink, and lust, and everything men thought wicked, and out of that celebration of iniquity he created a celebration of life itself. . . . [In the same way] *The Playboy* has inverted everything that is conventional in Ireland. And Synge could do this, which I think was his real work, because he was incapable of a political idea.[24]

Yeats has hoped to see Ireland turn from the bragging rhetoric, and deliberately seek a discipline and a unity by offering herself to her anti-self. In fact, his many-sided activities are dominated by his deep concern for the future of his country at 'the reversal of the gyres'. He was convinced that the dawn of a new subjective dispensation was about to break, and thought that his role was to prepare Ireland for the day she had to offer herself to her subjective ideal and attain that Unity of Being he perceived in Byzantium.

Because his system is largely deterministic, Yeats views history as 'necessity' which, when understood and accepted, may become the source of our 'freedom and virtue'.[25] The wisest policy for any nation is to learn where it stands in the recurrent cycle and to accept the inevitable, antithetical character of the phase in which it lives. Only in this way can it fulfil its destiny, and transform the necessity of history into liberty, making its 'chance at one with choice'. In *Pages From A Diary Written in Nineteen Hundred and Thirty*, he explains that 'we owe allegiance to the government of our day in so far as it embodies that historical being'.[26] Every age fashions from its opposite, and the great artist, being more receptive to the direction of the pre-ordained cycles than his fellow-countrymen, can re-create his nation by helping it find its true mask:

... I have found something hard and cold, some articulation of the Image, which is the opposite of all that I am in my daily life, and all that my country is; yet man or nation can no more make this Mask or Image than the seed can be made by the soil into which it is cast.[27]

This form of the Mask or Image comes from life and is fated; the artist, however, is concerned with the form that is 'chosen', for it is through his art that he has to impress upon the imagination of his people a vision of the new dispensation. The artist's 'business is not reformation but revelation',[28] and it is in this sense that Yeats sees his role as a nationalist in Ireland.

As all realization is through opposites, Yeats urges Irish poets to 'scorn the sort now growing up', and 'cast [their] mind on other days'[29] in order to hasten the demise of the present vulgar and materialistic age, and help Ireland not only to accept, but also to usher in, the imminent change. The world has grown weary of science and materialism, and 'there is so little in our stocking that we are ready at any moment to turn it inside out.'[30]

Perhaps now that the abstract intellect has split the mind into categories, the body into cubes, we may be about to turn back towards the unconscious, the whole, the miraculous; according to a Chinese sage darkness begins at midday. Perhaps in my search, as in that first search with Lady Gregory among the cottages, I but showed a first effect of that slight darkening.[31]

The new civilization will proceed out of all of us collectively, not out of some apocalyptic animal, or Mary's inhuman conception, or Christ's empty tomb, or any other void. It will be initiated by 'those who inhabit [our] "unconscious mind" and are the complement or opposite of that mind's consciousness.'[32] In other words, all that is cast out of this scientific, Christian, democratic era will be justified in the era to come.

Accepting the double nature of all things, Yeats could never free himself from double allegiance. No sooner did a feeling or an idea engage his attention, than it automatically threw up its opposite. He explained this process in one of his letters: 'I . . . see things double — doubled in history, world history, personal history.'[33] Existing among antithesis, he was full of that strength that guards against convictions by employing one against the other, and reserving freedom for himself. As Frank O'Connor put it, 'With one half of his mind he created the illusion but the other half remained critical and detached. That was what . . . saved him from pompousness, insolence, and fanaticism.'[34] He had a matchless power of identifying himself simultaneously or alternately with one cause and its opposite. He was an aristocratic nationalist, a middle-class Protestant, a Southern Unionist, a member of the I.R.A., an anti-clerical conservative, an autocrat, a pacifist, a fascist, an anarchist — but he could never wear any one of these masks for long. He used them whenever he thought they could help him bring about the Ireland he dreamt of, the unity of culture he hoped to establish, the Byzantium he wanted to re-create in twentieth-century Dublin. Like many great artists, he was only really interested in, or absorbed by, what was of use to his work, what could, in often strange and oblique ways, stimulate and inspire him. As soon as he got out of a political pose all that was grist to the mill, he dropped it, as was his way when something had served its purpose. In old age, as he tells us himself, he was 'unfit . . . for all politics but his own.'[35] He appealed to the Cellars and Garrets in Dublin to put an end to their heated debates and adopt his political beliefs as the most suitable for Ireland:

I suggest to the Cellars and Garrets that though history is too short to change either the idea of progress or the eternal circuit into scientific fact, the eternal circuit may best suit our preoccupation with the soul's salvation, our individualism, our solitude.[36]

Yeats's spiritual beliefs and political persuasions were utterly involved together and could not be separated. His intermittent political activities were nothing more than attempts to turn his personal *mythus* into a national mythology, and to relate it significantly to the Irish and European contexts. For him, therefore,

Unity of Being and Unity of Culture were not stylistic arrangements of experience conjured by the imagination of a poet, but real, practical politics. He seriously believed in the feasibility of reviving this kind of ideal society which existed in Europe from the eleventh to the thirteenth centuries. In 1921, he wrote to Lady Gregory, 'I would prefer to stay out of Ireland till my philosophy is complete and then to settle there and apply its doctrine to practical life.'[37] In the same year he wrote to George Russell from Oxford:

> I hope you will do that essay on Unity and Culture. . . . If we can present this one idea from many sides we might affect the future of Ireland! . . . politics being dead. . . . We should be the first to express the idea of unity in a practical form. . . . This conception of unity and culture has become a cardinal principle in all exposition of the future in my system. I am most anxious not to appropriate the idea or seem to do so. If I only express it it will seem but a deduction from one man's unpopular system. They will say "O that is Yeats" and pass it by. You spoke it all long ago and I would like to hear you speak it again . . . so that men can act upon it. . . . We writers are not politicians, the present is not our charge but some part of the future is.[38]

His primary concern at the time was to 'help the two Irelands, Gaelic Ireland and Anglo Ireland so to unite that neither shall shed its pride.'[39] He was certain that national literature should grow out of the history and experience of both communities, and hoped to wed the contemplative Catholic mind to the Protestant sense of form in order to achieve, through the marriage of contraries, that Unity of Being which is the supreme condition of life — a condition to which the individual soul and the nation ought to aspire. It was this right balance between Celtic 'thirst for unbounded emotion' and the Protestant tradition of discipline and public service which prompted his lifelong admiration for Lady Gregory. She belonged by birth to the Anglo-Irish gentry and by taste and instinct to 'the people' among whom she did her work on folklore and drama. He saw in her house the best of both worlds, the two conflicting halves brought together in perfect harmony and balance. In his introduction to her book, *Gods and Fighting Men*, he wrote:

> Old writers had an admirable symbolism that attributed certain energies to the influence of the sun, and certain others to the lunar influence. To lunar influence belong all thoughts and emotions that were created by the community, by the common people, by nobody knows who, and to the sun all that came from the high disciplined or individual . . . mind. I myself imagine a marriage of the sun and moon in the arts I take most pleasure in; and now bride and bridegroom but exchange, as it were, full cups of gold and silver, and now they are in a mystical embrace.[40]

In order to persuade Irish writers to make their work an organic function of their country's history, he was later to advance his theory of 'the conflict or union of races':

> The battle of the Boyne overwhelmed a civilization full of religion and myth, and brought in its place intelligible laws planned out upon a great blackboard; a capacity for horizontal lines, for rigid shapes; buildings, attitudes of mind that could be multiplied like an expanding bookcase. . . . It established a Protestant aristocracy some of whom neither called themselves English nor looked with contempt nor dread upon conquered Ireland. . . . The newest arrivals soon intermarried with an old stock, and the older stock had intermarried again and again with Gaelic Ireland. . . . Ireland, divided in religion and politics, though the last division began to disappear ten years ago, is as much one race as any modern country.[41]

With remarkable determination, the poet set out to remake the Irish nation to fit, as it were, the specifications of his planned unity. In setting up the Abbey Theatre, in reviving Irish mythology, and in his insistence on a symbolic drama, he was largely motivated by a genuine desire to bind together the segments of Irish society through that 'unity of image' which constituted the subjective equivalent of their history.

> If we would create a great community — and what other game is so worth the labour? — we must recreate the old foundations of life . . . as they must always exist when the finest minds and Ned the beggar and Seán the fool think about the same thing, although they may not think the same thing about it.[42]

He was intensely excited by the prospect of organizing a theatre that would establish a secret symbolical relation between the mysteries of the Irish Mystical Order and the modern mystery and miracle plays he intended to write. Hoping that his Dublin audiences could share the great emotions that only heroes can act upon, he began writing for the Abbey his recreations of ancient Irish myths. He was certainly interested in drama as the most hopeful way of putting the ideals of his movement before the people, and of bringing the urban populace back into line with the passionate heroes and storied folk:

> [The Abbey's] income was mostly from six-penny and one shilling seats. . . . Clerks, shop boys, shop girls and workmen — audiences of much enthusiasm but little money — came to see our plays, which appealed to them. Our theatre had its beginnings not among the rich . . . but right in the masses of the people. The working people showed the way and now . . . all classes come to us. . . .[43]

He wrote to a friend in 1908, 'Ireland's Drama must win the man in the street if it is going to be any use.'[44] He expected every spectator in his theatre to find himself, his neighbour, and indeed the whole Irish tradition. Unity, he believed, could only come to those whose lives are rooted in tradition; the wealthy find it in their 'Big Houses', and the peasants find it in the history of the earth. The urban populace, however, were traditionless; they lacked that sense of permanence that could save them from the vulgarity and materialism exported to Irish territory as a by-product of English rationalism and mechanical logic. This new class knew the world through abstractions, generalisations, statistics, time-tables, through images that refuse to compose themselves into a common design. No class can attain the condition of unity if it cannot

Share in . . . "the spiritualisation of the soil" — a doctrine derivable . . . from the truth that all emotional unities find their definition through the image, unlike those of the intellect, which are defined in the logical process. . . . I understand by "soil" all the matter in which the soul works, the walls of our houses, the serving-up of our meals, and the chairs and tables of our rooms, and the instincts of our bodies. . . .[45]

Behind this vision, of course, was a genuine political desire to bring about an Ireland that was the imagined wish-created opposite of the rational, unhierarchical Anglo-Saxon England. He believed that there was hope for Ireland to find itself by rising up against the earnestness, the logic, the timidity, and the commercialism of its conquerors. Its only salvation was to provide a homeland for the imaginative, the passionate, and the non-materialistic.

However, as we all know, his attempts to de-anglicise and de-commercialise Ireland failed because the Dublin middle classes were not co-operative. Contrary to what many people like to think, Yeats hated the middle class neither out of snobbery, nor out of some vaguely formulated belief that the mercantile classes have dimmed the vitality and romance of the world. During his 1903–04 American tour, for example, he praised the American middle class, who pared and saved to send their children to college, understanding that their country offered all forms of wealth and power to the disciplined mind. In a letter to Lord Dunsany he describes the middle class in the United States as 'so potent because it is so magnificent, with Whitman for its bard and Roosevelt for its man of action,' and adds, 'Ireland or at least Dublin is in the grasp of another kind of mediocrity; it is sordid and repulsive and issues from the cynicism of the slum.'[46] There is no doubt that Yeats's vigorous attack on intellectual philistinism was a lifelong struggle against a particular type of mentality that all artists castigate. However, those who attribute Yeats's quarrel with the middle classes in Ireland solely to his personal experience with the hysterical mobs at the Abbey, to the mass-intolerance in the Lane Affair, or to the attacks of Sinn Féin, miss a clear understanding of his system and oversimplify his position. His anger, in fact, is directed not so much against people in a particular income group as against those who perpetuate what he calls the 'conspiracy of the subconscious.'[47] If his contempt is more frequently directed against what we call the middle class, it is simply because the term is a convenient designation for those people who are relatively more susceptible to the flaws of contemporary life than anybody else in Ireland. 'The word "bourgeois" which I [used],' he once wrote, 'is not an aristocratic term of reproach, but like the older "cit" which one finds in Ben Jonson, a word of artistic usage.'[48]

Yeats maintains, as basic tenets of his system of *A Vision*, that the actual world is intersected by a spiritual one, and that the human soul would not be conscious were it not suspended between contraries. To him, therefore, human life is an endeavour to come to a double contemplation, that of the chosen Image, that of the fated Image. He stresses contemplation of the *Mask* and *Body of Fate* as the aim of his vision, for only through this twin contemplation can we catch a glimpse of the timeless individuality. Yeats's fury is, therefore, directed against those whose imagination has gone dead, whose experience is restricted to a single vision. When the senses are dulled by fact, the eye is fixed on the observed world, man cannot assume any other reality, and is trapped in the natural and unspiritual world. The mind of the new middle class tends to simplify by shearing away one aspect of reality, by blocking one side of the antinomies. It is marked by a total surrender of the antithetical, a 'continual adaptation to new circumstances of a logical sequence.'[49] Because of this adaptability their mind 'can be turned in any direction . . . is driven to all that is freakish or grotesque. . . .'[50] People who possess this kind of mentality can only seek, according to *A Vision*, the 'Unity of Fact by a single faculty, instead of Unity of Being by the use of all. . . .' Such people suffer from a 'gradual separation of *Will* and *Creative Mind*, *Mask* and *Body of Fate*,'[51] and their memory of the Unity of Being is dead. Once separated from their 'genius', they float upon the stream, are meaningless apart from time and circumstances, and their minds become a thoroughfare for others' thoughts. To such people, image and symbol are hateful, for they can only identify with their surroundings — their surroundings perceived as fact. In other words, the poet identifies the middle class with realism, rationalism and materialism — the civilization of the subconscious.

Yeats fully accepts Blake's doctrine that 'corporeal reason' binds us to mortality because it binds us to the senses, and divides us from each other by showing us our clashing interest; but imagination divides us from mortality, and binds us to each other by opening the secret door of the hidden life. In his own words:

> ... men who ate from the Tree of Knowledge wasted their days in anger against one another, and in taking one another captive in great nets; men who sought their food among the green leaves of the Tree of Life condemned none but the unimaginative....[52]

Yeats's characterization of the new middle class was further determined, in a variety of ways, by the symbolism of the system of *A Vision*. Since he often thought of the interpenetrating cones of the gyres in terms of sexual relations, he liked to imagine that fixation on a single cone, to the exclusion of the other, was bound to lead to a deprivation which is the intellectual equivalent of castration. Having repressed antithetical reality, the middle classes suffered a similar repression of their passions and their generative powers; they became hostile to sexuality and creativity. With hatred, instead of love, as the only energy they could cultivate, 'they contemplate all creative power as the eunuchs contemplate Don Juan as he passes through Hell on the white horse.'[53] The poet pondered further the correspondence between repressed imagination and repressed sexuality:

> Hate must, in the same way, create sterility.... Hatred as a basis of imagination, in ways which one could explain even without magic, helps to dry up the nature and make sexual abstinence, so common among young men and women in Ireland, possible. This abstinence re-acts in its turn on the imagination, so that we get at last that strange eunuch-like tone and temper.[54]

It is not surprising perhaps that in later years Yeats attributed much of his own renewed poetic activity to the Steinach rejuvenation operation.

To the mechanism, pragmatism and Puritan zeal of the middle classes, Yeats opposes what he calls the 'wasteful virtues': reverie, leisure, ease, passionate life and solitary contemplation. His ideal Irishman, therefore, is similar in many ways to the old heroes of Irish legend. In the world of Irish epics, the aristocrat, the hero, and the visionary are one. Cuchulain, the Irish hero Yeats admired most, combined the role of warrior, aristocrat, and visionary whose search for wisdom makes a complete unity of being possible. It is precisely this combination of worldliness with the capacity for visionary experience, the ability to hold the opposites in harmony and balance, which distinguishes the Yeatsian hero from the public hero of Carlyle, for example. Carlyle's hero is great because he is true to the needs of others and 'useful' to his fellow-men. Yeats condemns the author of *On Heroes and Hero-Worship* because of his 'ill breeding and theatricality'.[55] Yeats's hero is a self-born man who 'overcomes himself, and . . . no longer needs . . . the submission of others, or . . . conviction of others to prove his victory. . . . the sanity of the being is no longer from its relation to facts, but from its approximation to its own unity.'[56] His aristocratic hero pursues pure aimless joy,[57] for heroism accomplishes nothing, and exists only for its own sake — a far cry, incidentally, from the 'heroic vitalism' of the fascist hero. According to Yeats, the hero's courage in his struggle against necessity is the guarantee of his own spiritual worth. The more intense is his yearning for reality, the more does he understand that the objects of his desire do not exist in the physical world. Thus, he is driven to seek them in the dream world, and having found them there, he fashions the primary self into their expression. It is through passion — which Yeats defines as the straining of man's being against some obstacle that obstructs its unity — that the hero becomes conjoint to his buried self, and attains that wisdom which exceeds all book learning. In a very real sense, therefore, Yeats's class distinctions are primarily based on spiritual pedigree, or what he calls in 'The Man and the Echo', the 'spiritual intellect'. He envisaged an aristocracy of the spirit, with rank and social position only as a sort of adjunct or sequel.

Yeats's preference for the 'wasteful virtues' is not a red flag — something with which to make offensive gestures against the middle classes. He values the life of 'leisure', for example, because the mill of modern materialism has made awareness of metaphysical reality totally impossible. Leisure makes contemplation, 'reverie', or the free play of spiritual energies possible. 'The uneconomic leisure of scholars, monks and women gave us truth, sanctity and manners.'[58] In one of his Senate speeches he states, 'I am of the opinion of the Ancient Jewish book which says "there is no wisdom without leisure." '[59] As a matter of fact, Yeats is partial to the saint, the aristocrat, the hero, the peasant, the fisherman, the poet, the fiddler, the monk, the tinker and the old age pensioner because by discipline, privilege, profession, or habit they enjoy some kind of leisure which enables them to see the world as an object of contemplation, and to deepen their awareness of the spiritual reality. He writes in *A Vision*:

> The sense for what is permanent, as distinct from what is useful, for what is unique and different, for the truth that shall prevail, for what antiquity called the sphere as distinct from the gyre, comes from solitaries or from communities where solitaries flourish....[60]

If we examine 'leisure', 'excess', 'recklessness', and all the other enlarging virtues, we soon discover that they are not without some important spiritual significance. We are often told, for example, that Yeats's long visits to Coole Park and his friendship with Lady Gregory prompted his aristocratic pose, and that some of the aristocratic attributes he applauded were drawn directly from Castiglione's book, to which he was introduced by Lady Gregory. The poet had actually learned from Blake and Samuel Palmer, years before reading *The Courtier*, to reject timidity and tepid moderation. In his introduction to *The Poems of William Blake*, he quotes with obvious satisfaction his favourite poet: 'the roadway to excess leads to the palace of wisdom.'[61] He also recalls what Samuel Palmer wrote in 1824: 'Excess is the essential vivifying spirit, vital spark, embalming spice of the finest art.'[62] As a matter of fact, excess sharpens the opposition between man and daimon, rouses the will to intensity, and is an essential condition if unity is to be achieved. The Yeatsian hero (Cuchulain, Seanchan, Paul Ruttledge) is always in conflict with the conventional codes of society; and excess helps him to rise above the natural or social world to confront a supernatural reality. Recklessness, on the other hand, arises spontaneously from his mind when it sees itself exempt from death and decay, responsible to its source alone.

To Yeats, wealth and privilege were created only to free the mind, in part, from the material worries and to place those who possess them above the fear of life. However, he also realized that poverty, having nothing to lose, induced the same kind of detachment, the same kind of freedom from material reality. He never believed, as some would have us think, that the heroic, aristocratic mind was the monopoly of a small, elitist group. He defined his attitude to people, whether they were peasants or poets, philosophers or fiddlers, according to their imaginative and spiritual capabilities. For example, in 1902 he explained that the Celtic peasants 'had always ... for a supreme ritual that ... dance among the hills or in the depth of the woods, where unearthly ecstasy fell upon the dancers, until they seemed the gods or the godlike beasts ... and ... imagined for the first time in the world the blessed country of the gods and the happy dead.'[63] And when he adds that 'Folk-art is, indeed, the oldest of the aristocracies of thought',[64] we plainly see that his definition of aristocracy had nothing to do with position or social rank. He describes, for instance, the poet Blake, the old Fenian John O'Leary, the philosopher Whitehead, and his uncle Pollexfen as having aristocratic minds, while Bertrand Russell, John Locke and Thomas Carlyle are 'plebeians'.

In *The King's Threshold*, King Guaire values reason over imagination, logic over dream, and despite his royal blood, Yeats has no reluctance in reducing him to the level of his bourgeois mayor — both typify the 'new commonness' that rules the world. In one of his letters he describes Conchubar, the High King, as 'reason that is blind because it can only reason because it is cold';[65] he is a solid bourgeois man, timid, prudent, with a shrewd perception of main chance; the Blind Man is his shadow. Constance Markievicz, the daughter of a 'Big House', carried arms in Easter Week; and Yeats deliberately leaves her name from the roll of honour at the end of his poem 'Easter 1916'.

On the other hand, the leaders who planned the Easter Rising belonged to the class that Yeats hated and despised. But because these men have been 'changed utterly' in their violent encounter with the supernatural, he elevates them out of their 'common rut' and gives them heroic proportion. They achieve unity in the mask of the revolutionary martyr and become heroes, worthy associates of Emmet and Tone and the warrior-aristocrat Cuchulain himself.

The difference between the Ireland Yeats had dreamt of and the unheroic Ireland he saw developing around him, frustrated and disenchanted him. At the bottom of it all was the Gaelic-Catholic predicament: the rising Catholic middle class, in spite of its disapproval of English culture and English values, remained quasi-anglicised in its keen desire to achieve material prosperity through industrialisation. Castigating the vulgar and materialistic Anglo-Saxons, it persistently pursued the fruit of the culture it avowedly despised and condemned. Yeats was finally convinced that Dublin could not become Florence or Urbino in his lifetime and so he concluded: 'We can achieve Unity of Culture for a small number of people and leave it till the moon bring round its century.'[66] It was this kind of statement which perhaps prompted people like George Orwell and others in the 'forties to accuse him of reaching fascism by the aristocratic route. If Yeats believed in the inherited glory of a small elite, it was simply because he adhered to a spiritual, rather than a fascist, hierarchy based on the belief that the Higher Self in man grows and advances to loftier perfection by means of the experiences gathered by its successive incarnations on the physical plane. In other words, his ideology is based on a firm belief in metempsychosis, a belief which makes his authoritarianism totally different from that of the fascists. If we accept for a fact that Yeats believed in the rebirth of the soul and in some kind of karmic evolution, it would be immoral on his part to consider privilege, rank, beauty or wealth as accidents of birth:

> We're but given what we have earned
> When all thoughts and deeds are reckoned,
> So it's plain to be discerned
> That the shades of holy men
> Who have failed, being weak of will,
> Pass the Door of Birth again. . . .
> They are not changed to anything
> Having loved God once, but maybe
> To a poet or a King
> Or a witty lovely lady.[67]

The soul, according to the Celts — as Yeats learned early in his life — underwent a physical evolution from the soul-atom to mankind, then upward from a slave to a King on his throne. Physical beauty and spiritual perfection, like social rank, are earned through discipline, toil and evolution in life after life. The soul's perfection is always expressed in terms of physical loveliness: a lovely shell houses a perfect soul in phase 15 and the Unity of Being is expressed in terms of a well-proportioned body.

> How many centuries spent
> The sedentary soul
> In toils of measurement
> Beyond eagle or mole
> Beyond hearing or seeing . . .
> To raise into being
> That loveliness? . . .
> What death? What discipline? . . .
> What wounds, what bloody press,
> Dragged into being
> This loveliness?[68]

To Yeats the material and spiritual orders are inseparable; one 'ascending scale' links the goal and rewards in both. In *On the Boiler* he writes: 'As intelligence and freedom from bodily defects increase, wealth increases in exact measure. . . .'[69] He supports his theory with reference to the new science of eugenics, quoting at length from the tracts circulated by the eugenics societies in England. In occult science, too, he tells us in *A Vision*: 'the tradition is found which declares even to our own day that Christ alone was exactly six feet high, perfect physical man.'[70] It follows then that the function of the poet, as he sees it in 'Under Ben Bulben', is to 'bring the soul of man to God,/Make him fill the cradles right'.[71] Like the Platonists, he believed that matter is plastic and the soul makes it a receptacle for itself: 'The soul has a plastic power, and can . . . mould [the body] to any shape it will by an act of the imagination'[72] between one incarnation and another.

Genealogically speaking, Yeats's political ideology is rooted in a mixture of Celtic, Neoplatonist, medieval, Renaissance, and Indian philosophies, rather than in any modern fascist theory. He favoured the Neo-Platonists' emanation-theory which arranged all living beings into a hierarchy according to criteria such as 'degrees of perfection', 'power of soul', or 'realization of potentialities'. The antecedents of his doctrine can also be traced back to the sub-lunary and celestial divisions of the medieval chain of being which correspond to Yeats's interlocking cones; the medieval ladder of being is his Tower with its winding stair. It is not surprising, therefore, to find Yeats using in his political pamphlet, *On The Boiler*, a long quotation from Burton's *Anatomy of Melancholy* to support his main contention.

It is only possible, then, to speak of Yeats as a fascist or a social reactionary by ignoring the spiritual dimension of his historical and political views. We can readily understand why he disliked certain aspects of democracy which he saw as an egalitarian movement, a levelling process which admits of no relation between social, physical, and spiritual degrees. When he wrote in *On The Boiler* of 'the caste system that saved the intellect of India',[73] he was almost certainly thinking of Ireland too. The people of any nation, though they are all thrusting forward in the same direction, cannot be at the same point on the spiritual ladder. However, all who preserve tradition will find their opportunity in the end:

When we are moved to intolerance by some provincial folly or stupidity, one should look at the man or woman and think: "From that blood may yet come some man of genius, perhaps the saviour of a race. That stupidity may be even necessary to his being."[74]

In an essay addressed to Lady Gregory, Yeats wrote, 'Ireland has suffered more than England from democracy, for since the Wild Geese fled who might have grown to be leaders in manners and in taste, she has had but political leaders.'[75] He was convinced that the English parliamentary system threatened to establish on a permanent and virulent basis the divisions of opinion that are natural to the Irish way of thinking and prevent for all time his hopes for unity. His disparagement of democracy and his awareness of its shortcomings, however, do not mean that he pinned his hopes on Fascism.

In fact, Fascism was no closer to his ideal state than democracy. What excited Yeats most was not Mussolini's rise to power nor his astonishing utterances, but the fact that European thought seemed to be reversing itself as he had predicted. Any agreement with his theories, real or imaginary, excited him and renewed his faith in the system of *A Vision*:

> When I was under thirty it would seem an incredible dream that 20,000 Italians, drawn from the mass of the people, would applaud a politician for talking of the "decomposing body of liberty," and for declaring that his policy was the *antithesis* of democracy. Everything seems to show that the centrifugal movement which began with the Encyclopaedists and produced the French Revolution . . . has worked itself out. . . . Now we are at the beginning of a new centripetal movement. . . . The astonishing thing about Mussolini's utterances is not that he should think or say those things — other men have thought them before — but that he should be applauded for saying them. We may see the importance of that without admiring Mussolini. . . . One observes the change in European thought as one observes the day changing into night or the night changing into day.[76]

When he was asked in the same interview what he hoped a new authoritarian government would accomplish in Ireland, he could only think of his old dream: 'I shall be a very old man if I live to see [such a government] capable of taking up the tasks for which I care and of which I dream. . . . One of them certainly is to make a Dublin as worthy of our new Parliament as the great buildings, like the Bank of Ireland, were worthy of the old one. . . . I should like to see the best teaching in architecture, in metal work, in mosaic work. . . .'[77]

His momentary interest in fascism was centred in its spiritual and philosophical origins, and its possible corrective influence on the flounderings of a democratic society. In this connection, Joseph Hone writes: 'My memory goes back to a morning in Rome spent in searching the book-shops with Mrs. Yeats for works dealing with the spiritual antecedents of the Fascist revolution.'[78] Yeats also admired the philosophy of Giovanni Gentile, Mussolini's minister of education, so much that he selectively moulded some of Gentile's thought to make it resemble his own.[79] On one occasion he quoted with great satisfaction Gentile's view that 'the external world is so improbable, that we go along touching it with our own hands to convince ourselves that it exists.'[80] Above all, he found Gentile's advice to the Italian teachers to avoid the dry and abstract, to correlate all subjects of study, and to teach the whole curriculum as if it were one lesson, the closest thing to his cherished Unity of Being and Culture.

After the rise of Fascism in Italy and Nazism in Germany, however, he continued to be pessimistic about the future. 'The old age of our civilization,' he wrote, 'begins with young men marching in step, with the shirts and songs that give our politics an air of sport.'[81] He persisted in saying that this age 'is a road and not a resting place', and that Ireland had to prepare itself for the next revelation, the next turn of the wheel. He wrote to Olivia Shakespear that he was searching out signs of the whirling gyres of historical cones in occult books, and that by studying them he hoped to see deeper into what is to come. 'My own philosophy,' he explained, 'does not much brighten the prospects so far as any future we shall live to see is concerned. . . .'[82] By 1936 he had rejected politics altogether and had no faith in any form of modern government: '. . . why should I trouble about communism, fascism, liberalism, radicalism, when all . . . are going down stream with the artificial unity which ends every civilization? Only dead sticks can be tied into convenient bundles.'[83] By the time he wrote his poem 'The Gyres', his pessimism was even more profound: the atmosphere of the poem is one of destruction, chaos, and terror. 'The irrational streams of blood . . . staining the earth' point to a cosmic cataclysm; positive deliverance can only come from the great cyclical energy of the gyres. In 1935 Ethel Mannin and Ernst Toller tried to persuade him to take a definite position against totalitarianism. In answering them he wrote:

. . . my horror at the cruelty of governments grows greater. . . . Communist, Fascist, nationalist, clerical, anti-clerical, are all responsible according to the number of their victims. I have not been silent; I have used the only vehicle I possess — verse. If you have my poems by you, look up a poem called *The Second Coming*. It was written some sixteen or seventeen years ago and foretold what is happening. I have written of the same thing again and again since.[84]

The implication is that while 'The Second Coming' is a direct prophecy of imminent Fascist disaster, the chaos has its place in his system. Increasingly Yeats had learned that the antithetical age for which he longed might come only after the immersion in a darker and more turbulent period; it seemed to be the destiny of those who lived in the last quarter of our era which he described as 'The purging away of our civilization by our hatred.'[85]

The poet evidently rejected what he called the 'attempted unity by force'[86] in Nazi Germany and Fascist Italy. In a direct reference to the dictators in both countries, he explained that the time would come when thought would be unified as its own free act:

. . . we wait till the world changes and its reflection changes in our mirror and an hieratical society returns, power descending from the few to the many, from the subtle to the grosser, not because some man's policy has decreed it but because what is so overwhelming cannot be restrained. A new beginning, a new turn of the wheel.[87]

He predicted that at the end of our cycle 'civilization itself an instant before . . . its transformation . . . may . . . submit not to this or that external tyrant but to a Being or an Olympus all can share.'[88] In short, the unifying and organizing force may be some ideal, a spiritual discipline which imposes order from within.

The Fascist views were slowly unfolding in the 'thirties; and the excesses of the Italian regime simply confirmed Yeats's natural hostility to all existing forms of government. Under the Italian dictator, for example, indications of a faith in numbers, an uncritical emphasis on quantity irrespective of quality, was beginning to emerge. In *On The Boiler*, Yeats violently denounced the Fascists in Europe for sponsoring large families. In this respect they were no better than the Bolshevists:

The Fascist countries . . . because they must feed their uneducatable masses, put quantity before quality; any hale man can dig or march. They offer bounties for the seventh, eighth, or ninth baby, and accelerate degeneration. In Russia . . . the stupidest man can earn a bounty by going to bed. . . .[89]

He also rejected the avowed intention of the Fascists to abate class struggle as one way of combating Communism. In the strange document he called 'The Genealogical Tree of Revolution',[90] Yeats divided modern thought into two main streams—the Fascist and the Marxist, representing two ways of resolving the antinomies — and posed a third possibility which was his own view, and which was based upon his belief that the antinomies cannot be resolved. He believed that the Fascists were wrong to reduce the struggle within the individual and the society because in his opinion intellectual initiative and good taste were impossible without such a struggle. He added that both the dialectical materialism of Karl Marx and his school, and the modern philosophy of Italy, also influenced by Hegel, were inadequate. 'There is no final aim, neither the losing of the individual, class, nation in the whole, or the return of classes to the mass bringing their gifts.'[91]

Furthermore, Yeats rejected the Hegelian and the Fascist claim that the State is prior to ideology and that it is an end in itself. As he put it in 1921, 'In many ways a great State kills all under its shadow like a horse chestnut.'[92] He believed that the individual works out his destiny through the institutions of the state, but it is he (the individual), and not these institutions, who is the centre of gravity in the state. He felt that the principles on which the ideal state should be founded are 'Freedom, God, and Immortality',[93] adding that the first nation which can possess these three convictions will control the moral energies of the soul. He rejected totally the attempt of the Fascists and the Bolshevists to turn the idea of the corporate state into free powers: 'The idea of the State which is not a preparation for these three convictions, a State founded on economics alone, would be a prison house. A State must be made like Chartres Cathedral for the glory of God and the soul.'[94]

In 1933 he wrote to Olivia Shakespear: 'We are about to exhaust our last Utopia, the State.'[95] He embodied his disaffection with the State in a poem written in 1934:

> What if the Church and the State
> Are the mob that howls at the door![96]

Yeats was basically for *man* against *mob*, while the Fascists were for the *State* against *man*. His aim was unchanging: a harmonious reconciliation of order and freedom in unity of culture because, as he said in On The Boiler: 'if we do not hold to freedom and form', the counter-Renaissance he expected 'will come, not as an inspiration in the head, but as an obstruction in the bowels'.[97] Yeats in fact was becoming painfully aware that the Fascist state was even cruder than a democratic state. He was beginning to realize that uniforms, whether they be Fascist or Marxist, suggest uniformity, loss of individual will, and rejection of the antithetical.

Yeats never sympathised with the Fascist politics of violence and war, and his revulsion from the growing murderousness of the world was forcefully expressed in his prose and poetry. When Mussolini finally translated his irredentism into a policy of imperial conquest with the Abyssinian Campaign in 1935, Yeats condemned this war without reluctance or reservation: 'All through the Abyssinian war,' he wrote, 'my sympathy was with the Abyssinians. . . .'[98]

It might be useful at this point to remind ourselves that in the late 'twenties and early 'thirties Fascism was new and fashionable and had certain respectability on account of its anti-Communism. And in fairness to the poet, we should remember that the British conservative press at the time welcomed Mussolini as the energetic saviour of Italy from Communist revolution, a champion against socialism. In July 1934 *The Times* wrote that in the years ahead there was more reason to fear for Germany than to fear her. *The Daily Mail* gave its unqualified support to Mosley and the British Union of Fascists. Winston Churchill met Mussolini in 1927 and praised those who backed Fascism against the Reds.

Let us go back a few years to say something of Yeats's shortlived cordiality to the Blueshirts, which has been misinterpreted as an attempt to promote a Fascist movement in Ireland. There is no space here to discuss this movement and its successor, the Catholic-Fascist Christian Front, at length. It may be sufficient to refer briefly instead to the assertions of Michael Tierney and James Hogan — the two minds behind the social and political doctrine of Blueshirtism — that this movement which had many of the external trimmings of Fascism, owed its inspiration first and foremost to the Papal encyclicals *Rerum Novarum* and *Quadragesimo Anno*.[99] The corporate state of the *United Ireland* intellectuals was no mere reproduction of Mussolini's Italy. It was the vocational teaching of Pope Pius XI which they sought to put into practice, and to do that, as Professor Tierney wrote, it was 'not in the least necessary to share Mussolini's rather drastic and in some ways excessive views on the exclusive right of the state.'[100] The obvious Catholicism and anti-Communism of the Blueshirts immediately won them the support of the business classes, the confidence of the Catholic hierarchy, and even the trust of the British Government. The movement was regarded as the answer to the Bolshevik heresy on the one hand, and the older individualist heresy of materialist *laissez-faire* on the other. The objectives of the movement were common to many Irish political parties at the time, and Yeats, like almost everyone else in the country, was worried by the leftist leanings of the I.R.A. To use his own words, he wanted 'to keep Ireland from giving itself (under the influence of its lunatic faculty of going against everything which it believes England to affirm) to Marxist revolution and Marxist definition of value in any form.'[101] Yeats, who had praised the 'rule of kindred' as the impending form of government, believed that corporations or professional groupings of persons engaged in the same trade were as natural as the family grouping. As the individual in his personal and spiritual life is associated with the family, so in his larger, or social and economic life, he would be naturally associated with the larger family of the corporation. In the first edition of *A Vision* (1925), he writes:

When the new era comes . . . it must awake into life . . . organic groups, covens of physical or intellectual kin melted out of the frozen mass . . . a world resembling . . . that of the Greek tribes — each with its own daimon or ancestral hero.[102]

By advocating such a policy, Yeats was not aiming at a dictatorship; he was simply bringing up to date, so to speak, the medieval guild system or promoting the Indian caste-group government of which he learned so much from Shree Purohit Swami in the 'thirties. The truth of the matter is that the corporate form of society is not wedded historically or politically to any particular form of government. In *On the Boiler* he points out that it has its antecedents in the distant past: 'The Far East has dynasties of painters, dancers, politicians, merchants, but with us the dancer may be the politician's mother . . . the painter his rebellious son.' [103] By family or race, Yeats means any group which is a kindred of any kind as distinct from an organized opinion, any entity held together, not by logical process, but by historical association. In his attempt to restore the authority of the family, he suggests that the members of any family are joined by a bond so powerful that they form a common gyre; they meet again and again in life after life.[104] Furthermore, he viewed the social order in terms of two alternating struggles:

[The] social order is the creation of two struggles, that of family with family, that of individual with individual, and . . . our politics depend upon which of the two struggles has most affected our imagination. If it has been most affected by the individual struggle we insist upon equality of opportunity, "the career open to talent," and consider rank and wealth fortuitous and unjust; and if it is most affected by the struggle of families, we insist upon all that preserves what that struggle has earned, upon social privilege, upon the rights of property.[105]

Yeats who makes Cuchulain's life in *On Baile's Strand* 'like a bird's flight from tree to tree', rejecting family and clan, understands at the end of his life that man 'stands between two eternities, that of his family and that of his soul.' [106]

The poet expected the Blueshirt movement to be different from its Italian counterpart, for he hoped that it would express the genius of Ireland as he understood it. He was assured by his close friend Captain Dermot MacManus, the organizer of the movement, that it was about to, or might be persuaded to, espouse his 'Unity of Being' and turn it into a discipline, a way of life. The poet had no reason to doubt MacManus's word or his qualifications; he was not only a serious student of oriental mysticism but was also gestating at the time a book on Irish fairies. Yeats describes him in one of his letters as 'an old friend of mine, served in India, is crippled with wounds . . . and therefore dreams an heroic dream.' [107] We are also told that he had cured himself by oriental meditation,[108] a few months before he arranged the meeting between Yeats and General O'Duffy, the man he chose to lead the Blueshirts. MacManus explained to the poet that O'Duffy was a 'simple peasant' and could be prevailed on to adopt most of Yeats's ideas. Yeats reported the arrangement to Olivia Shakespear in July 1933:

> ... the Fascist organizer of the blue shirts had told me that he was about to bring to see me the man he had selected for leader that I might talk my anti-democratic philosophy. I was ready, for I had just rewritten for the seventh time the part of *A Vision* that deals with the future.[109]

When General O'Duffy came to his house, Yeats expatiated on Hegel and Spengler, but the General's intellectual qualifications were scarcely such as would arouse the poet's enthusiasm. O'Duffy was unsubtle, muddleheaded and contradictory; all he could report, as he came out of the interview, was that he got the poet to promise him some songs. The interlocutors were obviously at cross-purposes and Yeats wrote, soon after their encounter: 'He seemed to me a plastic man but I could not judge whether he would prove plastic to the opinions of others ... or to his own ... "Unity of Being".'[110] The poet, as his letters at the time indicate, was neither impressed nor excited by O'Duffy's personality. However, since Cosgrave, head of the pro-Treaty party, proved moderate in opposition, Yeats hoped that the General's organization would sharpen opposition and perhaps, by way of a strenuous struggle, restore 'heroic politics' to Ireland. Though he remained on the fringes of the movement, an uncommitted but amused observer, for a few months, he kept his word and wrote the songs for O'Duffy's men.

The marching songs themselves were not in the least demagogic; one of them is actually directed against fanaticism:

> Those fanatics all that we do would undo;
> Down the fanatic, down the clown;
> Down, down, hammer them down ... .[111]

It took Yeats only a few months to discover that he could not seriously associate with this crew. By the autumn of 1933, he was describing the mob tactics of O'Duffy as a 'political comedy'. The General himself was a demagogue, a 'mechanical toy',[112] for his movement took its cue from the fanatics the poet had condemned in his song. The chasm between his ideals and those of the Blueshirts soon prompted him to ridicule their efficient ruthlessness and humourless dedication:

> "Drown all the dogs," said the fierce young woman,
> "They killed my goose and a cat.
> Drown, drown in the water-butt,
> Drown all the dogs," said the fierce young woman.[113]

Only one year after his interview with General O'Duffy, Yeats regretted having written these songs:

Because a friend belonging to a political party wherewith I had once some loose associations, told me that it had, or was about to have, or might be persuaded to have, some such aim as mine, I wrote these songs. Finding that it neither would nor could, I increased their fantasy, their extravagance, their obscurity, that no party might sing them.[114]

He does that simply by making the marching feet those of a supernatural army. And, three years later, he expresses a genuine fear that the O'Duffy volunteers, on their return from the Spanish war, would threaten the life of his ' "pagan" institutions, the Theatre, the Academy'.[115]

At the end of his life, we find Yeats thoroughly disgusted with all political organizations and disenchanted with all forms of government. In 1936 he writes: 'as my sense of reality deepens, and I think it does with age, my horror at the cruelty of governments grows greater. . . .'[116] However, to say that he ever abandons his belief that unity of culture is practicable or attainable, would be untrue. He assures himself of the validity of his Utopian dream by praising, in his last prose work, the only two examples that he thought approximated to the ideal government he had been striving, for half a century, to create in Ireland: the Swedish system of government, and the Indian caste-group government. 'One nation,' he declares in On the Boiler, 'has solved the problem. . . . Plato's Republic with machines instead of slaves may dawn there. . . . Sweden has spent on education far more than the great nations can afford. . . .'[117] He explains that the Swedish Court, a family beloved and able, has gathered about it not the rank only, but the intellect of the country, satisfying 'a need of the race no institution created under the influence of English . . . democracy can satisfy.'[118] The love of Stockholm and belief in its future 'so filled men of different minds, classes, and occupations that they almost attained the supreme miracle, the dream that has haunted all religions. . . .'[119]

He found his other example in the East, exemplified by Sato's sword and by Tagore's poetry, where a tradition which has passed through centuries, gathering from learned and unlearned metaphor and emotion, carried back again to the multitude the thought of the scholar and the nobleman. This kind of culture remained unbroken because, as Yeats tells us, it went

> From father unto son
> And through the centuries ran
> And seemed unchanging like the sword.
> Soul's beauty being most adored,
> Men and their business took
> The soul's unchanging look. . . .[120]

From Shree Purohit Swami, with whom he associated closely for four years, Yeats learned of the Hindu adherence to a unique system which believed both in retributive metempsychosis and the rule of kindred. The Hindu caste system is governed by rules of descent, rules of marriage, ritual, occupation and ideas about purity and pollution. Both in *On the Boiler* and in *Purgatory* he reveals a strong bias in favour of the Indian caste system which runs counter to the tenets of modern democracy, for it prohibits the pollution of endogamous groups, and links caste with occupation.

Something should be said here of Yeats's last mask, his final stance: in his anger and despair he openly professed a mixture of wild anarchism and bitter gaiety. In a letter to Ethel Mannin, decrying the deceit and moral cowardice of modern politics, he wrote: 'As a young man I used to repeat to myself Blake's lines: "And he his seventy disciples sent/Against religion and government."'[121] He assumed the mask of the 'Wild Old Wicked Man' who was 'Bound neither to Cause nor to State',[122] for whom government and morality were of no account. Deeply convinced that our cycle of civilization was nearing its end, he felt that any hope for Unity of Culture must await the advent of the new antithetical dispensation. The only reasonable thing to do under the circumstances was to hasten the collapse of the old dying order. 'Some day you will understand . . . why I can be no other sort of revolutionist,' he wrote to Ethel Mannin, 'my rage and that of others like me seems more important. . . . we may but be the first of the final destroying horde. . . .'[123] In another letter he stated categorically, 'I am a forerunner of that horde that will someday come down the mountains.'[124] In *On the Boiler* he insisted that we accept war gaily, as a means of hastening the transformation: 'Love war because of its horror, that belief may be changed, civilization renewed.'[125] His writings plainly anticipate the furious passion of the antithetical unicorns that will trample the old order to death and provide the energy for building a new and vigorous kind of Spartan civilization, which he associates with joy and ecstatic laughter. Towards the end of his life he wrote, 'All I wanted was impossible, and I wore out my youth in its pursuit, but now I know it is the mystery to come.'[126] It is not surprising, therefore, that his epitaph looks forward to the fulfilment of his dreams; his hopeful expectation that the 'fierce horsemen' will ride again inspired him to address it to those who have mastered the elegant harmony of existence, those who can view with cold detachment the realities of life and death.

Appendix: Genealogical Tree of Revolution

I

Nicholas of Cusa

Kant Restates the Antinomies

Hegel Believes that He has Solved Them with his Dialectic

Thesis : Antithesis : Synthesis

All Things Transparent to Reason

II

DIALECTICAL MATERIALISM
(Karl Marx and School)

a] Nature creates Spirit.
Brain creates Mind.
Only the reasonable should exist.
Evolution.

b] Dialectic as conflict of classes.
Each class denied by its successor.
History, a struggle for food; science, art, religion, but cries of the hunting pack.

c] The past is criminal.
Hatred justified.
The Party is above the State.

d] Final aim : Communism.
Individual, class, nations lost in the whole.

e] The Proletariat justified, because, having nothing, it can reject all.

III

ITALIAN PHILOSOPHY
(Influenced by Vico)

a] Spirit creates Nature.
Mind creates Brain.
All that exists is reasonable.
Platonic reminiscence.

b] Dialectic rejected.
Conflicts are between positives ('distincts').
Civilisation, the rise of classes and their return to the mass bringing their gifts.

c] The past is honoured.
Hatred is condemned.
The State is above the Party.

d] Final aim : Fascism.
Individual, class, nation a process of the whole.

e] History, now transparent to reason, justified.

IV

A RACE PHILOSOPHY

The antinomies cannot be solved.

Man cannot understand Nature because he has not made it. (Vico.)

Communism, Fascism, are inadequate because society is the struggle of two forces not transparent to reason — the family and the individual.

From the struggle of the individual to make and preserve himself comes intellectual initiative.

From the struggle to found and preserve the family come good taste and good habits.

Equality of opportunity, equality of rights, have been created to assist the individual in his struggle.

Inherited wealth, privilege (sic), precedence, have been created to preserve the family in its struggle.

The business of Government is not to abate either struggle but to see that individual and family triumph by adding to Spiritual and material wealth.

Materially and Spiritually uncreative families or individuals must not be allowed to triumph over the creative.

Individual and family have a right to their gains but Government has a right to put a limit to those gains.

If a limit is set it must be such as permits a complete culture to individual and family; it must leave to the successful family, for instance, the power to prolong for as many years as that family thinks necessary the education of its children.

It must not be forgotten that Race, which has for its flower the family and the individual, is wiser than Government, and that it is the source of all initiative.[127]

Needless Horror or Terrible Beauty

1. *The Collected Poems of W. B. Yeats* (London : Macmillan, 1967), p. 214.
2. *Ibid.*, p. 330.
3. *Ibid.*, p. 101 and 392.
4. *Mythologies* (London : Macmillan, 1959), p. 301.
5. *The Collected Poems of W. B. Yeats*, p. 233.
6. J. Hone, *W. B. Yeats 1865-1939* (London : Macmillan, 1962), pp. 458-9.
7. A. Wade, *The Letters of W. B. Yeats* (London : Rupert Hart-Davis, 1954), p. 600.
8. *W. B. Yeats: Memoirs*, ed. Denis Donoghue (London : Macmillan, 1972), p. 216.
9. *On the Boiler* (Dublin : Cuala Press, 1939), p. 20.
10. *A Vision* (New York : Macmillan, 1972), p. 52.
11. *The Variorum Edition of the Poems of W. B. Yeats* (New York : Macmillan, 1957), p. 791.
12. *Poems of William Blake* (Cambridge : Harvard University Press, 1969). p. xliv.
13. G. Keynes (ed.), *The Complete Writings of William Blake with All Variant Readings* (London : OUP, 1957), p. 149.
14. *Essays and Introductions* (London : Macmillan, 1961), p. 103.
15. G. M. Harper, *Yeats's Golden Dawn* (New York : The Macmillan Press, 1974), p. 79.
16. *Pages From a Diary Written in Nineteen Hundred and Thirty* (Dublin : Cuala Press, 1944), p. 20.
17. *The Collected Poems of W. B. Yeats*, p. 283.
18. *Autobiographies* (London : Macmillan, 1955), p. 183.
19. Israel Regardie, *The Golden Dawn: An Account of the Teachings, Rites and Ceremonies of the Order of the Golden Dawn* (Minnesota : Llewellyn Publications, 1969), Vol. I, p. 26.
20. S. L. MacGregor Mathers, *The Kabbalah Unveiled* (New York : Samuel Weisner, 1970), p. 52.
21. R. Ellmann, *Yeats: The Man and the Masks* (London : Faber and Faber, 1961), p. 100.
22. F. Farr, G. B. Shaw, W. B. Yeats: *Letters*, ed. C. Bax (Dublin : Cuala Press, 1941), p. 51.
23. *Yeats and the Occult*, ed. G. M. Harper (Toronto : Macmillan of Canada, 1975), p. 195.
24. *The Collected Poems of W. B. Yeats*, p. 78.
25. *Ibid.*, p. 73.
26. *The Letters of W. B. Yeats*, p. 503.
27. *The Variorum Edition of the Plays of W. B. Yeats*, ed. Russell K. Alspach (New York : The Macmillan Company, 1966), p. 1071.
28. *Ibid.*, p. 1097.
29. *The Collected Plays of W. B. Yeats* (London : Macmillan, 1966), p. 381.
30. *A Vision*, p. 74.
31. *Ibid.*, pp. 143-4.
32. *Yeats and the Theatre*, ed. R. O'Driscoll and L. Reynolds (Toronto : Macmillan of Canada, 1975), p. 76.

33 *Ibid.*
34 *On the Boiler*, p. 30.
35 *Yeats: The Man and the Masks*, pp. 248-9.
36 *The Collected Poems of W. B. Yeats*, p. 233.
37 *Ibid.*, p. 225.
38 *Ibid.*, pp. 230-31.
39 *Ibid.*, p. 430.
40 *The Collected Plays of W. B. Yeats*, pp. 259-66.
41 *Ibid.*, p. 162.
42 *Mythologies*, p. 189.
43 *The Variorum Edition of the Poems of W. B. Yeats*, pp. 469-70.
44 *A Vision*, p. 268.
45 *The Collected Poems of W. B. Yeats*, p. 241.
46 *A Vision*, p. 250.
47 *Ibid.*, p. 105.
48 *Yeats and the Occult*, p. 220.
49 *The Variorum Edition of the Plays of W. B. Yeats*, p. 1160.
50 *The Collected Plays of W. B. Yeats*, p. 339.
51 *The Collected Poems of W. B. Yeats*, p. 332.
52 *Autobiographies*, p. 123.
53 *Pages From A Diary Written in Nineteen Hundred and Thirty*, pp. 1-2.
54 *On the Boiler*, p. 15.
55 *The Collected Poems of W. B. Yeats*, p. 231.
56 *Ibid.*, p. 234.
57 *Pages From A Diary Written in Nineteen Hundred and Thirty*, p. 57.
58 *The Collected Poems of W. B. Yeats*, p. 358.
59 *Wheels and Butterflies* (London: Macmillan, 1934), pp. 109-110.
60 *The Collected Poems of W. B. Yeats*, pp. 398-9.
61 *Autobiographies: Reveries Over Childhood and Youth and The Trembling of the Veil* (New York: Macmillan, 1927), p. 339.
62 *Essays and Introductions*, pp. 518-9.
63 *Autobiographies: Reveries Over Childhood and Youth and The Trembling of the Veil*, p. 473.
64 *On the Boiler*, p. 30.

W. B. Yeats and the Politics of *A Vision*

1 *The Poetry of W. B. Yeats* (London: Oxford University Press, 1941).
2 'Passion and Cunning: An Essay on the Politics of W. B. Yeats' in *In Excited Reverie*, ed. A. Norman Jeffares and K. G. Cross (London: Macmillan, 1965), pp. 207–78.
3 *The Collected Works in Verse and Prose* (Stratford-upon-Avon, 1908), vii, 3.
4 *The Words Upon the Window Pane* (Dublin: Cuala Press, 1934), p. 1.
5 *Explorations* (London: Macmillan, 1962), p. 137.
6 Richard Ellmann, *Yeats: The Man and the Masks* (London: Faber and Faber paperback, 1961), p. 249.
7 *On the Boiler* (Dublin: Cuala Press, 1939), p. 13.
8 Allan Wade, *The Letters of W. B. Yeats* (London: Rupert Hart-Davis, 1954), p. 219.

Notes on the text

9. *On the Boiler*, p. 37.
10. *Ibid.*, p. 13.
11. *The Collected Poems of W. B. Yeats* (London : Macmillan, 1967), p. 365.
12. *Essays and Introductions* (London : Macmillan, 1961), p. 526.
13. *Ibid.*, p. 193.
14. Frank O'Connor, 'The Old Age of A Poet', *The Bell*, February 1941, p. 16.
15. *Pages from a Diary Written in Nineteen Hundred and Thirty* (Dublin : Cuala Press, 1944), p. 2.
16. *Mythologies* (London : Macmillan, 1959), p. 366.
17. *Wheels and Butterflies* (London : Macmillan, 1934), pp. 108–09.
18. *Autobiographies* (London : Macmillan, 1955), p. 195.
19. *Essays and Introductions*, p. 402.
20. *Explorations*, p. 144.
21. *Ibid.*, pp. 158–59.
22. *Essays and Introductions*, p. 255.
23. *On the Boiler*, p. 15.
24. R. O'Driscoll, 'Yeats on Personality : Three Unpublished Lectures' in *Yeats and the Theatre*, ed. R. O'Driscoll and L. Reynolds, (Toronto : Macmillan, 1975), pp. 47–49.
25. *Pages from a Diary Written in 1930*, p. 54.
26. *Ibid.*, p. 33.
27. *Autobiographies* (London : Macmillan, 1926; New York : Macmillan, 1927), p. 339.
28. *The Collected Plays of W. B. Yeats* (London : Macmillan, 1966), p. 378.
29. *The Collected Poems of W. B. Yeats*, p. 400.
30. *The Letters of W. B. Yeats*, p. 812.
31. *Explorations*, p. 404.
32. *A Vision* (New York : Macmillan, 1972), p. 237.
33. *The Letters of W. B. Yeats*, p. 887.
34. 'The Old Age of a Poet', *The Bell*, Feb. 1941, pp. 14–15.
35. Notes to 'Three Songs to the Same Tune', *The Spectator*, 23 February 1934.
36. *Explorations*, p. 355.
37. Richard Ellmann, *Yeats : The Man and the Masks*, p. 245.
38. *The Letters of W. B. Yeats*, pp. 665–67.
39. *Pages from a Diary Written in 1930*, pp. 54–55.
40. *Gods and Fighting Men* (London : John Murray, 1905), p. xix.
41. *The Words Upon the Window Pane*, pp. 5–6.
42. *Explorations*, p. 28.
43. John P. Frayne and Colton Johnson (eds.), *Uncollected Prose : Later Reviews, Articles and Other Miscellaneous Prose, 1897–1939* (London : Macmillan 1976; New York : Columbia University Press, 1976), Vol. II, p. 403.
44. Irish Literary Theatre MSS., National Library, Dublin (Letter, 11 May, 1908).
45. *Explorations*, p. 273.
46. Unpublished letter in the Berg Collection (52B 0636), New York Public Library.
47. *Autobiographies* (1927), p. 327.

48 Denis Donoghue (ed.), *W. B. Yeats: Memoirs* (London: Macmillan, 1972), pp. 168–69.
49 *A Vision*, p. 155.
50 Ibid., p. 156.
51 Ibid., p. 162.
52 *Essays and Introductions*, p. 130.
53 *Estrangement* (Dublin: Cuala Press, 1926), p. 29.
54 Ibid., pp. 30–31.
55 *Essays* (London: Macmillan, 1924), p. 291.
56 *A Vision*, p. 127.
57 *The Collected Poems of W. B. Yeats*, p. 158.
58 *Pages from a Diary Written in 1930*, pp. 52–53.
59 *The Senate Speeches of W. B. Yeats* (London: Faber, 1961; Bloomington: Indiana University Press, 1960), p. 39.
60 *A Vision*, p. 300.
61 *The Poems of William Blake*, edited and with an introduction and notes by W. B. Yeats (London: Lawrence and Bullen, 1893), p. xlii.
62 *Essays*, p. 151.
63 *Essays and Introductions*, p. 178.
64 *Mythologies*, p. 139.
65 *The Letters of W. B. Yeats*, p. 425.
66 *Pages from a Diary Written in 1930*, p. 55.
67 *The Collected Poems of W. B. Yeats*, p. 127.
68 *The Collected Plays of W. B. Yeats*, pp. 281–82.
69 *On the Boiler*, p. 18.
70 *A Vision*, p. 273.
71 *The Collected Poems of W. B. Yeats*, p. 399.
72 *Essays*, pp. 514–15.
73 *On the Boiler*, p. 19.
74 *W. B. Yeats: Memoirs*, p. 155.
75 *Explorations*, p. 257.
76 *Uncollected Prose*, Vol. II, p. 434.
77 Ibid., p. 435.
78 J. Hone, *W. B. Yeats 1865–1939* (London: Macmillan, 1962), p. 368.
79 See *A Vision*, p. 81.
80 Hone, *W. B. Yeats 1865–1939*, p. 376.
81 G. M. Harper, *Yeats and the Occult* (New York: Macmillan, 1975), p. 218.
82 *The Letters of W. B. Yeats*, p. 668.
83 Ibid., p. 869.
84 Ibid., p. 851.
85 Ibid., p. 825.
86 Ibid., p. 887.
87 *Pages from a Diary Written in 1930*, p. 55.
88 Ibid., p. 32.
89 *On the Boiler*, p. 19.
90 See Appendix.
91 Hone, *W. B. Yeats 1865–1939*, p. 468.
92 *The Letters of W. B. Yeats*, p. 666.

93 *Pages from a Diary Written in 1930*, p. 52.
94 Ibid.
95 *The Letters of W. B. Yeats*, p. 813.
96 *The Variorum Edition of the Poems of W. B. Yeats* (New York: Macmillan, 1957), p. 554.
97 *On the Boiler*, p. 27.
98 *The Letters of W. B. Yeats*, p. 872.
99 M. Manning, *The Blueshirts* (Toronto: University of Toronto Press, 1971), pp. 211–31.
100 Francis MacManus (ed.), *The Years of the Great Test* (Cork: The Mercier Press, 1967), p. 49.
101 *The Letters of W. B. Yeats*, p. 656.
102 *A Vision*, (London: privately printed by Werner Laurie, 1925), pp. 213–14.
103 *On the Boiler*, pp. 12–13.
104 *A Vision*, p. 237.
105 *Explorations*, p. 270.
106 *Letters On Poetry to Lady Dorothy Wellesley* (London: Oxford University Press, 1940), p. 182.
107 *The Letters of W. B. Yeats*, p. 813.
108 W. B. Yeats and Margot Ruddock, *Ah, Sweet Dancer: A Correspondence*, ed. Roger McHugh (London: Macmillan, 1970), p. 32.
109 *The Letters of W. B. Yeats*, pp. 812–13.
110 Ibid., pp. 813–14.
111 *The Variorum Edition of the Poems of W. B. Yeats*, p. 544.
112 *The Letters of W. B. Yeats*, p. 815.
113 *The Variorum Edition of the Poems of W. B. Yeats*, p. 546.
114 Ibid., p. 837.
115 *The Letters of W. B. Yeats*, p. 885.
116 Ibid., p. 851.
117 *On the Boiler*, p. 19.
118 *Autobiographies*, p. 572.
119 Ibid., p. 556.
120 *The Collected Poems of W. B. Yeats*, p. 228.
121 *The Letters of W. B. Yeats*, p. 873.
122 *The Collected Poems of W. B. Yeats*, p. 223.
123 *The Letters of W. B. Yeats*, p. 869.
124 Ibid., p. 873.
125 *On the Boiler*, p. 20.
126 *Pages from A Diary Written in 1930*, p. 28.
127 A. N. Jeffares, *W. B. Yeats: Man and Poet* (London: Routledge and Kegan Paul, 1962), pp. 351–52.